D0756443
2001603500

PROMISES

Bad Boy
by Barbara Catchpole
Illustrated by Sarah Horne
Published by Ransom Publishing Ltd.
Unit 7, Brocklands Farm, West Meon, Hampshire GU32 1JN, UK
www.ransom.co.uk

ISBN 978 178591 252 8
First published in 2016

A CIP catalogue record of this book is available from the British Library.

Bad Boy

Barbara Catchpole

LFC
GEOLOGY
ROCKS
3

1

Hi! My name is Taylor and I hate boys!

No, OK, only joking!

But are they human – like us? Are they from the same universe?

I reckon they come from a galaxy far, far away.

Listen up. Let me tell you about my horrible boyfriends.

Kevin

I met Kevin at church.

He asked me out by accident.

His gran was yakking to my gran about potatoes (no, I don't know either) and Kevin suddenly said, 'Do you want to go out?'

He meant go out 'in the fresh air' but I didn't get it.

So suddenly Kevin had a girlfriend. And **NO CLUE** what to do with her.

Kevin owned three computers, a smelly T-shirt with 'Geology rocks!' on it, and a giant spider called Birdie.

Why was it called 'Birdie'? You don't want to know!

He collected rocks.

His friends all looked at me as if a girl was a strange animal they had never seen before.

I suppose that is possible!

I used to sit there on the sofa in his damp and nasty basement with five geeky boys staring at me.

It was like being a giant panda.

I gave up on supergeek after two weeks – but he didn't notice for another

GEOLOGY
ROCKS

week because he never left his computer screen. Three weeks then. A record!

Brad

Then there was Brad.

Brad owned three Liverpool shirts which he wore all the time.

He probably wore them in bed.

He probably wore them in the bath.

He would have worn all three at once if he could.

He only ever watched football. He only ever talked about football. He only ever ate red food!

I must tell you this! On Valentine's Day he sent me a home-made card. It said:

Arsenal is red
Chelsea is blue
I love Liverpool
And I love you a bit too!

LFC

So romantic!

He lasted two and a half weeks.

I broke up with him on a Wednesday because I couldn't face another Saturday.

Kirk

Then there was Kirk.

Now this wasn't Kirk's fault. He had allergies.

The terrible thing was that Kirk was allergic to anything with a perfume.

Which basically meant he was allergic to girls.

I mean, I must spray or dab or rub about twenty different smells onto my body and face every day. Every hour, sometimes.

Poor old Kirk would sniff.

Then he would start sneezing – and not just little sneezes. Oh no, these were great big Sneeze Explosions.

TISSUES
UP
NOSE

I won't describe it, it was gross!

We got thrown out of the cinema after he sneezed down some fat guy's neck.

We had to break up after he had a really bad attack and had to be taken to hospital.

I reckon if we had ever kissed, it would have killed him.

I think he might have to go and live in a bubble in Iceland or something.

Anyway, that one was two weeks and fifty-seven packets of tissues.

Ollie

Then there was Ollie, who was … well, how can I put this nicely?

I know! I won't bother! Tell it like it is, girl!

Stupid.

Ollie was really, really stupid.

He looked really good, but he was like one of those cheap Easter Eggs – just a thin layer of chocolate over absolutely nothing.

We were in Homebase, right, and I said I liked bonsai, and he said he didn't know I was into martial arts!

Then we were in McDonalds and he asked for a cheeseburger without any cheese.

He was too stupid to know that he was stupid.

3
m

It was sad.

It lasted about a month, because whenever I said, 'I think we should break up,' he would say 'Duh - break up what, Taylor?'

Steve

Finally – Steve.

Steve chewed gum all the time. And I mean **ALL** the time.

His mum said he chewed it in his sleep, but I reckon that would be dangerous.

Or maybe he'd had so much practice he could do it OK.

(Did he wake up in the night to change to a new piece of gum? *Go for a pee, update gum.* Gross!)

Anyway, the first time he kissed me, the gum ended up in my mouth. Mega-gross!

One week, if you're wondering.

Now those boys all sucked at being a boyfriend.

My Josh isn't like that at all.

He looks amazing.

He is quite tall but not freaky, you know? His shoulders are wide – he works out!

His hair is dark and it sort of gets in his eyes.

And his eyes – his eyes are a deep chocolate brown and he has this way of

JOSH

raising just one eyebrow when he asks a question.

OK, I'm a lost cause!

He is downright, drop dead, heart goes thump, thump, thump gorgeous.

Can I say that bit again?

He is downright, drop dead, heart goes thump, thump, thump gorgeous.

I am going to tell you all about him. But there is one thing you must understand before I go on with my story.

Josh looks good and I love him, but he is a very bad boy.

Bad to the bone.

I'm not going to say that bit again.

2

Everybody hates my boyfriend.

Well, not everyone – but loads of people.

My dad can't stand him. My dad

hasn't liked any of my boyfriends.

He's very fair like that.

Still, he can't stand Josh and it's much more than that whole Arsenal / Spurs thing.

Ginny (my bestie) and her Ginger Freak boyfriend don't like him.

The teachers certainly don't like him – last to lessons and first out the door, lippy and sulky, no homework, no pen but shed-loads of attitude. Tie undone and shirt out!

That's my Josh!

Only the art teacher likes him and she just sees him as a walking A* grade.

On the days he's not late to school, he skives off and plays video games.

Even his mum doesn't seem to like him much, or she'd cook him a hot meal or wash his stuff from time to time.

You see, he hangs around with the wrong sort of people. He comes from one of those big tower blocks on the estate.

I don't like his friends very much and I've told him so.

I don't like fighting and I don't like gangs.

It's hard for Josh though. It's where he lives, you know?

Those are the people he has grown up with and he and his brothers hang out with them.

Still, things have got to change.

I'm going slowly, though. Boys have

to think things through for themselves before the girl tells them what to do. You have to pretend they are the boss!

So how did we get together?

Well Josh 'stalked' me. No, really he started to follow me round in school and 'pop up' next to me.

He was next to me in the dinner queue.

He sat next to me in assembly.

He chose my activity on Activity

Day and actually came to school that day.

He even went to the library.

As if Josh ever read a book! Well, not one that wasn't on mending motorbikes.

I can still see him standing there reading 'The Hobbit'. Upside down (the book, not him!).

Finally he asked me to go and see a film with him.

It was a horrible film, with loads of people dying, getting shot and splattering blood everywhere.

I think half the actors died in the first five minutes.

Of course, Josh loved it.

Then we walked back across the rec and we just didn't stop talking.

We lay on that closed-in roundabout thing and watched the stars go round and he kissed me, just once, and I think I knew that we were meant to be together.

It was a brilliant evening – apart from the blood splatter.

That was five months ago and now we see each other every day.

Even the teachers know we're together and they say things like, 'Tell that boyfriend of yours he's in the team!'

I've got plans for the future, too.

I'm really into nail art and it's what I'm going to do when I leave school.

I do loads of people's nails and they pay me a bit as well, although I do some of Gran's friends for free.

Josh is an amazing artist, although all he likes to draw is motorbikes. Perhaps he could design tattoos.

Perhaps we could have a nail art and tattoo shop and get a flat together somewhere nice.

Perhaps … perhaps …

I can't tell you what, but I had dreams. And I was going to make them come true.

Then it all went wrong.

3

'Have you heard about the big gang fight on the estate?' Ginny asked me at lunchtime.

I felt sick.

Josh hadn't mentioned a fight and I had only seen him at break.

'I bet Josh will be there.'

She popped a bit of brown mushy stuff into her mouth. 'Peter says all the estate guys are going'

– like I cared what the Ginger Freak said!

Josh was so **NOT** going!

I had to talk to him, so I headed to the art room.

Josh and Dwayne were doing an amazing pop art picture of different motorcycles done in hot neon colours.

Dwayne lives in the flat below Josh and they are buds.

They were spraying onto a stencil and didn't hear me come in.

'Dwayne, I need to talk to Josh!'

'And I need to get this finished!' Dwayne's a moron.

Josh just looked at him and he left.

'What do you want, Taylor?' His gorgeous mouth was sulky and he couldn't meet my eyes.

'You know what I want.'

'I was going to tell you.'

'When?'

'Soon.'

'Well, you're not going, Josh.'

Now, do you spot my mistake?

'I think I am.' He scowled.

I tried to get it back. 'Look, I know it's your choice, but Josh, it's so dumb. The police will be there. They read the 'posts'.

'I can't let my friends down. They are my people.'

That was when I lost it.

'We're not in some dumb American cop movie, Josh! They is not your "peeps"! Grow up! It is your choice! It's them or me! Choose!'

‘Look Taylor, everyone is going.’

‘Then everyone is as thick as you. Choose, Josh! Them or me!’

‘I’m going, Taylor.’ He pushed his hair back. ‘I’m not wimping out.’

‘Then I’m going too! Right out of your life!’

I was shouting by then and ran out, slamming the classroom door. Josh was left standing.

He suddenly opened the door and

shouted after me ‘You don’t own me, Taylor! You don’t own me!’

4

Saturday morning I was in our kitchen putting tiny little palm trees on our Tracy's toenails.

She's my cousin and I had just painted her toenails hot pink for her holiday. She's going to Benidorm at half term.

Now we were doing my favourite bit: little transfers.

She had wanted flamingos, but honestly, how daft is that?

They wouldn't show up on the pink, so she's having palm trees.

Gran was sitting drinking a mug of tea and Tracy was texting as I worked. Quite honestly that was a good thing, because she's a bit of a wriggle-bum.

'Hey, Taylor,' she said, 'everyone's posting about the fight on the estate. There's about fifty kids down there and everyone's there. Is your no-good boyfriend going?'

Gran was watching me. She has very bad eyes now, but she sees a lot – if you know what I mean.

I didn't know what to do.

I wanted to go down to the estate and beg him not to fight.

I hadn't gone to sleep at all last

night. I had just cried and thrashed about and got knotted up in my bed sheets.

My eyes were so puffed up I could hardly see the little palm trees.

I wanted to see him so badly, but I didn't want to make a fool of myself. He had made his choice and I had my pride.

'I like Josh,' Gran said quietly. 'The boy is an idiot, but he loves you, Taylor.'

That made up my mind.

'Gotta go!'

I had to get to him before he was hurt!

'What about my foot, Taylor?' Tracy said, 'Taylor! Taylor!'

But I was out of there.

I ran as fast as I could. I had to get to the subway that led to the estate.

Suddenly, in the distance, I could

hear the wail of police sirens. A guy came past me, running the same way.

Police sirens or ambulance?

I was out of puff and my ribs were hurting.

Then in my head I saw Josh , lying on the pavement, bleeding out.

I was stupid! Why oh why oh why didn't I stop him?

'Taylor!' he was calling to me, 'Taylor!'

Was it just in my head? I thought I could hear him.

I ran across the road to the top of the subway.

'Taylor!'

I turned to look as a white van came racing around the corner, heading for the estate. It hit me – thwump – and I was thrown sideways.

Then it was like time slowed down.

I couldn't breathe – just couldn't get

the air in. Darkness started to creep in the sides of what I could see.

I heaved, trying to get some air in, but it was no good.

And as everything went dark I heard Josh call again, but this time his voice was high, as if he were in pain.

'Taylor!'

As everything went black, I thought I felt his warm lips on mine.

5

It was still dark, but I could smell something. I knew that smell ... What was it?

It was hospital! I could smell hospital.

I tried to open my eyes, but it was like they were glued shut.

'Taylor!'

It was Josh's voice.

Why couldn't he leave me alone? I just wanted to go back to sleep …

'Wake up, love, please … '

My eyes popped open. It was so bright!

I was in a room, no, one of those

spaces with curtains. Josh was sitting next to me and my dad was standing in the corner, really giving him evil looks.

I was surprised Dad didn't chuck him out!

Then I really was staggered because Dad came over and kissed me and then went out so Josh and I could talk.

I tell you – when you are in hospital, everyone is nice to you. I should have asked for a pony!

'I thought you kissed me.'

'I tried to give you the kiss of life like on telly. The ambulance bloke had to pull me off you. I think he thought I was molesting you. He said you were breathing OK and would breathe a lot better if I kept my mouth off yours! I felt a right idiot!'

I laughed and it really hurt. Turns out two ribs were broken.

'But why were you there? I thought you were at the estate.'

He took a deep breath.

'I was coming to say 'sorry', wasn't I?'

I reckon saying that hurt him more than broken ribs!

'Say it then!'

He got up and put his arm around me.

'Get off – it hurts! My arm hurts too! Go on, say it!'

'I came back, didn't I? I felt bad … really bad. I can't make it without you,

Taylor. I can't sleep. I can't draw. I can't even watch telly.'

'But I don't own you – remember?'

'Maybe you do – a little bit.'

I reached out and touched his long black curls.

What was going on?

His big brown eyes filled with tears.

'I thought I'd lost you.'

'Not that easy to lose me.'

Maybe my guy wasn't so tough …

Maybe he wasn't so bad after all.

I still made him say 'sorry' though! He nearly choked, but he did it!

You know, I really think Josh is the one.

Yes, **THE ONE**.

More great reads in the Promises series

ch@t

by Barbara Catchpole

'Are you out of your tiny looney-tunes mind?'

That's what Gina's sister says when she finds out Gina is chatting online with a boy she doesn't know.

But Gina loves talking to Chatboy1 – he makes her laugh and he *understands* her. But what will happen when Gina tries to meet him IRL?

A Time to Live

by Sue Purkiss

It's 1942, during the Second World War, and France is occupied by the German army. These are dangerous times.

Sylvie Duval, 17, forms a close friendship with Jack, an injured British airman they are sheltering.

But Jack is in danger and he must leave France. Sylvie faces difficult choices as the man she loves prepares to be smuggled out of the country.